Twin Flames Under the Moon
"If Time Had Chosen Us"

By
Jennifer Montiel

Monarch Story House

First Edition
Printed in the United States of America

ISBN#

Content Warning

This novel contains themes and depictions that may be emotionally difficult for some readers.

Please be aware that this story includes references to:

- Domestic abuse
- Alcohol and substance addiction
- Post-traumatic stress disorder (PTSD)
- Infidelity
- Emotional neglect and unresolved attachment
- Serious injury and death in the line of duty
- Grief, loss, and mourning
- Mental health struggles
- Depictions of violence related to law enforcement work

These elements are presented within a reflective, character-driven narrative that explores the consequences of unresolved trauma, delayed choices, and emotional attachment.

This book does not romanticize abuse, addiction, or violence. Its purpose is to encourage awareness, self-reflection, and thoughtful consideration of personal choices and emotional well-being.

Reader discretion is advised.
If you or someone you know is struggling with similar issues, support from trusted individuals or professional resources is encouraged.

Law Enforcement Disclaimer

This novel portrays law enforcement work as part of a fictional narrative inspired by real experiences.

Procedures, timelines, and circumstances have been adapted, condensed, or dramatized for storytelling purposes and should not be interpreted as exact representations of police protocols, training standards, or operational practices.

This book is not intended to serve as a guide, manual, or instructional reference for law enforcement activity. Any resemblance to real events, procedures, or individuals is coincidental or used solely for narrative clarity.

AUTHORS NOTE

This novel is inspired by a true story lived quietly, shaped by real emotions, real consequences, and real time.

Names, locations, and certain details have been changed to protect privacy, but the heart of the story remains honest. The experiences explored in these pages reflect themes many people carry silently unresolved love, delayed choices, trauma, duty, and the cost of waiting too long.

This book was not written to glorify pain or romanticize suffering. It was written to examine how belief, fear, and silence can shape lives just as powerfully as action. It is also a reminder that strength does not always look like endurance, and love does not always mean staying.

If this story feels personal, it is because many of us have stood at the edge of a choice and hesitated.

My hope is that this novel encourages reflection, compassion, and clarity—both for ourselves and for others.

Thank you for reading with an open heart.

TABLE OF CONTENTS

Chapter One. San Solano	1
Chapter Two. The Rule	4
Chapter Three. Growing Quiet	7
Chapter Four. Leaving	9
Chapter Five. The Night She Stayed	12
Chapter Six. What Stayed Behind	15
Chapter Seven. What She Carried	17
Chapter Eight. Fallout	20
Chapter Nine. The Promise	23
Chapter Ten. Distance That Breathes	26
Chapter Eleven. Time Served	30
Chapter Twelve. What Remains	34
Chapter Thirteen. What Took Hold	37
Chapter Fourteen. Out of Alignment	40
Chapter Fifteen. The Mark	44
Chapter Sixteen. The Cost of Belief	48
Chapter Seventeen. The Confession	52
Chapter Eighteen. The Night We Tried to Let Go	56
Chapter Nineteen. After the Cut	60
Chapter Twenty. Almost	65
Chapter Twenty-One. What She Never Said Out Loud	69
Chapter Twenty-Two. Under a Full Moon	75
Chapter Twenty-Three. The Funeral	82
Chapter Twenty-Four. What Was Left Behind	88
Chapter Twenty-Five. No One Left to Carry It	92
Chapter Twenty-Six. What He Numbed	96
Chapter Twenty-Seven. The Envelope	100
Chapter Twenty-Eight. What Remains	108
Chapter Twenty-Nine. What People Call a Bond	112
Chapter Thirty. What Love Is Not	116
Chapter Thirty-One. The Lives That Continued	119

Dedication Page

For those who waited.

For the ones who loved quietly,
mistook patience for devotion,
and learned—sometimes too late—
that choosing yourself is not betrayal.

For the Selene's and the Adan's,
and for anyone still standing at the edge of a choice.

CHAPTER ONE

San Solano

San Solano stayed small on purpose. Streets curved back into themselves. Families blended early. Stories traveled faster than truth.

Selene met Adan before memory learned order.

Their mothers shared pregnancies. Appointments overlapped. Laughter filled waiting rooms. By the time Selene learned words, Adan already existed in her life.

He lived three streets away. Close enough to feel permanent.

Adan's mother, Mrs. Cindy White, stood near Selene's life from the beginning. She taught at the elementary school throughout her entire career. Generations passed through her classroom. Parents trusted her without question.

Selene passed through that classroom too.

There was no escaping Mrs. White's presence. At school. At church. In town. She watched without appearing to. She called it care.

Nothing happened between Selene and Adan.

That mattered.

They grew up in parallel. Same hallways. Same playgrounds. Same quiet awareness. Selene noticed him without knowing why. Adan noticed her without reaching.

San Solano watched them grow.

It always did.

One afternoon, Selene's mother, Maribel, picked her up from school and ran into Mrs. White near the front of the building. It had been a while since they last spoke without rushing.

"Life keeps us busy," Maribel said.

Mrs. White nodded. "Too busy."

"We should get together for dinner," Maribel said. "At my ranch. Let the kids play."

At the time, Mrs. White had three boys. Maribel had two girls. It felt simple. Familiar. Dinner was scheduled without hesitation.

Before leaving, Mrs. White looked at Selene. Not briefly. Not politely. She studied her.

"You've grown so much," she said.

Selene shifted under the attention, unsure why it felt heavy.

Maribel laughed easily. "Who knows," she said. "Maybe one day our kids are destined to get married. Trust me. I can see the future. It runs in generations."

Mrs. White didn't laugh.

Some people in town avoided Maribel. They whispered about her. They were afraid of what she might know. She had always carried a reputation. A special eye. An ability to see beyond what was spoken.

Maribel never denied it.

But she was careful with Selene.

"Never be ashamed," she told her later. "The future can be seen, but it can always be changed."

Dinner at the ranch came together easily.

Cars lined the dirt drive. Children ran without instruction. Laughter carried farther than it should have. It felt like the kind of night people remembered later and called simple.

Selene stayed close to her sister at first. Adan stood near his brothers. They didn't speak much. They didn't need to.

Adults talked around them. Stories overlapped. Plates were passed. Mrs. White watched the children the way she watched her classroom. Calm. Measuring. Always aware.

At one point, Selene and Adan found themselves near the fence line. Not alone. Just adjacent. Close enough to feel each other's presence without crossing into it.

Adan looked taller than she remembered. Quieter too.

They didn't touch.
They didn't smile.

But something shifted anyway.

Mrs. White noticed.
Maribel noticed too.

Nothing was said.
Nothing needed to be.

That night, Selene stood by her bedroom window and looked up.

The moon hung full and quiet in the sky.

Adan was part of her life before choice ever arrived.

And San Solano remembered everything.

CHAPTER TWO

The Rule

Adan's house always felt the same.

The living room smelled faintly of coffee and cleaner. Family photos lined the walls. School portraits. Sports teams. Holidays frozen in neat frames. Everything in its place.

Selene had been there her entire life. She didn't need directions. She knew which couch cushion dipped slightly in the middle. Which lamp flickered when it was turned on too fast.

Mrs. Cindy White sat in her usual chair near the window. Upright. Hands folded. Watching without appearing to.

Adan stood nearby, quiet as always. Present, but not interrupting.

Mrs. White spoke gently, as if the words were meant to comfort.

"I know you love him," she said.

The sentence landed without warning.

"And you are an amazing girl."

Selene felt her chest tighten. Compliments felt heavier when they came paired with limits.

"I love you as my goddaughter," Mrs. White continued. "You will always be welcome in my home. Always."

Selene nodded. She had learned early how to listen without responding.

"But I can never see you as his girlfriend," Mrs. White said. "And never as his wife."

Her voice did not change. She said it the way she delivered lessons. Calm. Certain. Final.

"You and him… it's wrong," she added. "We are family."

The word settled between them.

Family.

It was meant to sound protective. Wise. Like something Selene should accept with gratitude.

Adan did not look at her. He stared ahead, jaw tight, absorbing the rule the way he absorbed everything else. Quietly. Completely.

Mrs. White leaned back slightly, as if concluding something reasonable.

"If you really love him," she said, "you will let him be."

The sentence rearranged Selene's understanding of love.

Love, she realized, was being asked to disappear.

She nodded again. She always did.

After that, everything stayed the same—and nothing did.

Selene continued to come over. She sat on the same couch. She laughed at the same jokes. She ate dinner at the same table. But she learned where not to stand. How long not to look.

Adan followed the rule without question. He stayed close enough to feel familiar, far enough to feel unreachable. His silence became its own answer.

They never spoke about it.
They never tested it.

Rules like that didn't need reminders.
They lived inside you.

That night, Selene lay awake longer than usual. The house was quiet.
Her thoughts were not.

She stared out the window and felt the familiar pull rise again.
Instinct without instruction.

The moon sat high and full in the sky.

She didn't speak the words yet.

Some things take time to become language.

CHAPTER THREE

Growing Quiet

Adan's mother never kept them apart.

That was the part people didn't understand.

Selene and Adan went everywhere together. Family dinners. Birthdays. Church events. Holidays. They sat at the same tables and rode in the same cars. No one questioned it.

They went to prom together.

Not as a couple.

As something unnamed.
Something permitted but carefully defined.

Photos were taken. Smiles were practiced. Mrs. White stood nearby, watching with approval that never crossed into warmth.

They did absolutely everything together.

Except date.

That was the line.

Mrs. White called it respect. She called it tradition. She said they had grown up too close, like family, and family didn't cross certain boundaries.

"You both need to find your own paths," she said. "That's how you honor what we've built."

So they did.

They applied to different schools. Made separate plans. Talked about futures that never included each other out loud.

But they still met for dinner. Still showed up together. Still moved through rooms as if drawn by something quiet and constant.

Selene learned what it meant to be close without permission.

She noticed how people assumed things and then corrected themselves. How questions stopped halfway. How glances lingered and then moved on.

Adan accepted it all without complaint. He showed respect the way he'd been taught. By not pushing. By not asking. By carrying silence like responsibility.

Sometimes that hurt more than distance ever could.

During those years, the moon became Selene's habit.

On full nights, she stepped outside and looked up without explanation.

Hello, moon.

She wondered if Adan felt it too. If the same stillness found him wherever he stood.

They never spoke about it.

They didn't need to.

Some bonds are allowed everywhere—
except where they matter most.

CHAPTER FOUR

Leaving

The decision didn't arrive all at once.

It came in pieces. Conversations that started quietly. Plans spoken in halves. The kind of change adults make when they believe they're doing the right thing.

Maribel called it a new beginning.
A chance to start fresh.
A way to give her family more space than San Solano ever allowed.

Selene listened without interrupting. She nodded the way she always did when choices were already made.

They were moving.

Packing began slowly. Boxes stacked along the walls. Drawers emptied. Familiar things reduced to labels and tape. San Solano shrank as the house filled with evidence of leaving.

Adan found out the way everyone did. Casually. As if it were news and not an ending.

"You're moving?" he asked.

She nodded. "With my parents."

He didn't ask where.
He didn't ask when.
He didn't ask if she wanted to.

He already knew the answers didn't belong to him.

They still spent time together after that. Dinners. Long drives with the windows down. Quiet evenings where nothing needed to be said. Everything felt heavier, like the air itself was bracing.

Mrs. White approved of the move.

"Distance is good," she said. "It helps people grow into who they're meant to be."

Selene understood what she meant.

Distance made obedience easier.

On their last night, Adan drove his old pickup past the edge of town, where the road thinned and the fields opened wide. He cut the engine. Crickets filled the silence. The sky felt closer there.

They sat behind the truck, leaning against the tailgate. The grass pressed cool against their backs. Their shoulders nearly touched.

The moon rose full and unguarded.

Selene lifted her hand and pointed upward. "My mom says the moon holds power," she said. "That you can feel connection through it. That you can sense love, even when you're far away."

Adan studied the sky. "That's an interesting way to think about it," he said.

She hesitated, then went on.

"Let's do something," she said. "When we're apart."

He turned toward her.

"Whenever you see a full moon," she said, "remember me. I'll look up too."

She paused, then added softly, "It will help me feel less alone."

The words stayed between them. Honest. Unprotected.

Adan nodded slowly, like he was accepting something he didn't fully understand.

"I like that," he said. "I really do."

He leaned in and kissed her.

It wasn't rushed. It wasn't careless. It felt like agreement without definition.

When he pulled back, his forehead rested against hers.

"It won't be long," he said. "I heard my mom is thinking about moving too. A bigger city. Somewhere we can grow instead of staying stuck here."

Hope slipped into his voice before caution could stop it.

"You know I care about you," he said. "We won't be separated long."

Selene wanted to believe him. The moon watched quietly above them.

Later that night, Selene stood in her room, boxes stacked along the walls, everything half packed, and half remembered. She looked out the window and felt the familiar pull.

Hello, moon.

Morning came quickly.

Cars were loaded. Doors closed. San Solano watched without protest.

Selene didn't look back when they drove away. Some things are easier to carry forward than to leave behind.

CHAPTER FIVE

The Night She Stayed

Selene went back to San Solano for a weekend.

It wasn't planned as anything significant. A visit. Familiar faces. The comfort of a place that still knew her name.

Adan was there.

They ended up in his living room the way they always had. Late. Quiet. The house settled around them like it always did. The same couch. The same lamp casting soft light across the walls.

Nothing felt unusual.

Until it did.

Selene sat beside him at first. Close enough to feel his warmth. Close enough to feel the years press in. Conversation drifted into silence without either of them trying to stop it.

At some point, she shifted—almost without thinking—and ended up sitting on his legs. It felt natural. Familiar. Like something remembered by the body before the mind could intervene.

Adan didn't move away.

He rested his hands lightly at her waist. Careful. Uncertain. The kind of restraint that trembles under its own effort.

They looked at each other for a long moment.

Then they kissed.

It wasn't rushed. It wasn't reckless. It felt like something that had waited long enough to exist.

They didn't go any further.

They stayed like that. Holding each other. Breathing slowed. The night stretched in a way that felt separate from consequence.

At some point, sleep took them both.

Mrs. White saw them in the early hours of the morning.

Selene curled against Adan. His arms around her. Peaceful. Unaware.

Mrs. White stood in the doorway longer than necessary.

She said nothing.

She didn't wake them.
She didn't turn away.

She observed.

Morning came quietly.

Selene woke first. She disentangled herself carefully, as if movement alone might undo what had happened. She left the room without waking Adan.

Later that day, she found Mrs. White in the kitchen.

"I love your son," Selene said softly.

The words felt exposed. Honest. Like something that couldn't be taken back.

Mrs. White looked at her for a long moment.

Then she nodded once.

No approval.
No rejection.
No acknowledgment that anything had changed.

The silence was deliberate.

It closed the door without touching it.

Selene left San Solano later that day.

The memory stayed.

Some moments don't need permission.

But they always have consequences.

CHAPTER SIX

What Stayed Behind

Time did what distance always does.

Years passed.

Selene was gone, and life in San Solano kept moving the way it always had. Slowly. Predictably. Without ceremony.

Adan stayed.

The move his mother once spoke about never came. Plans shifted. Opportunities passed. Comfort settled in. Mrs. White remained rooted in the town that had shaped her.

Adan followed.

He met a girl his mother introduced him to. She was kind. Appropriate. Someone who fit easily into the life already arranged around him.

They spent time together. Then more. It felt expected.

When she became pregnant, Adan didn't hesitate. Responsibility arrived, and he accepted it the way he accepted everything else. Fully. Without resistance.

Marriage followed.

A son was on the way.

Adan built a life that looked like success from the outside. A career in banking. A stable home. A family people approved of. He became the kind of man others pointed to when they spoke about doing things the right way.

He told himself he was happy.

The days filled quickly. Work. Preparation. Obligation. There was little room left for memory. Even less for questions that didn't serve the present.

The moon still rose.

Sometimes Adan noticed it without knowing why. A pause. A flicker of something unfinished. But the ritual had lost its language. There were no words attached to the feeling. No one waiting on the other side of it.

The promise faded quietly.

Not broken.

Just unattended.

Adan didn't speak Selene's name anymore. He didn't look for her. He didn't ask himself where she had landed.

Life had moved forward.

And he moved with it.

Some things don't end in fire.

They end in forgetting.

CHAPTER SEVEN

What She Carried

Selene's life did not unfold gently.

She married young. His name was John Smith. He wore a uniform. He spoke with certainty. He promised safety and direction at a time when Selene didn't yet trust her own voice.

She learned obedience quickly.

When the anger came, she told herself it was normal. When the control followed, she assumed it was love. She did not question the treatment. She had been taught that endurance was virtue.

She survived by staying quiet.

The damage didn't stop when the bruises faded.

To dull the fear and confusion, Selene reached for what softened the edges of days she didn't know how to face. Alcohol first. Then drugs that made time feel less sharp. It wasn't rebellion. It was survival disguised as relief.

Addiction crept in quietly.

She functioned. She showed up. She hid it well enough to convince herself she was still in control. Nights blurred. Mornings arrived heavier. Shame followed close behind.

Even then, Adan surfaced in the back of her mind.

Not as a fantasy.

As a question.

Why did he forget about me?

Sometimes the thought arrived with resentment—toward him, toward his mother, toward the way obedience had shaped them both so differently.

One night, the violence went too far.

An old friend happened to visit. A familiar face at the wrong moment—or the only moment that mattered. He stepped in without hesitation. He got her out.

His name was Marco.

Marco didn't ask her to explain herself. He didn't demand a story that made sense. He recognized the addiction for what it was—not weakness, but a wound that had never been allowed to close.

He stayed.

Recovery didn't arrive all at once. It came in pieces. Setbacks. Long conversations. Days that demanded honesty instead of numbness. Marco walked beside her, not ahead of her. He helped her choose clarity when avoidance felt safer.

Slowly, Selene reclaimed herself.

When she spoke about becoming a police officer, Marco didn't doubt her. He didn't flinch at her past. He didn't treat her survival as something she owed him gratitude for.

Strength replaced coping.

Selene became a cop. A good one. Respected. Focused. Grounded. She built a life that belonged to her. She married Marco. They had a child together. Stability followed—earned, not promised.

Adan's image faded with time.

Mostly.

Except for one thing.

The moon.

On full nights, Selene still looked up. The ritual lingered, long after the meaning had thinned. She didn't speak his name anymore.

Hello, moon.

She assumed Adan's life had turned out the way his mother always described it. Perfect. Settled. Approved.

She didn't know the truth.

That the marriage was failing.
That misery lived quietly behind approval.

Some lies are passed down like tradition.

Selene didn't know he was heading for divorce.
She didn't know he was unraveling.

She only knew this:

Some loves fade.
Some transform.

And some survive as memory—
not destiny—
waiting only if you let them.

CHAPTER EIGHT

Fallout

Adan came to her city for work.

The message arrived without warning. A conference downtown. Two nights. A hotel Selene passed often but never noticed. Seeing his name again felt unreal, like something lifted from another life.

They agreed to dinner.

The restaurant was quiet enough to talk. Neutral. Safe. The kind of place meant for catching up without committing to anything else.

At first, conversation stayed light. Work. Time. How strange it felt to be sitting across from each other again. But memory has a way of slipping into gaps.

They started laughing about childhood. About San Solano. About the ranch. About the pickup truck and long drives that never went anywhere.

Adan shook his head, smiling. "What about your mom?" he asked. "Maribel. I guess her oracle wasn't right after all."

Selene smiled back, calm. "We're still alive, aren't we?"

He looked at her, curious.

"She can see the future," Selene said. "But she always told me we can shape it."

The words settled between them.

She pulled out her phone and showed him photos. Family gatherings. Her child. Her badge. Moments of pride she had earned the hard way.

Adan studied each one carefully. "You did good," he said quietly.

Then it was his turn. A picture of his son. Work achievements. A life that looked stable, respectable.

"I'm going through a divorce," he said after a pause. "It's almost done."

Selene felt something loosen inside her.

"There's something else," he added. "I'm joining the army."

She looked surprised.

"It's always been a dream," he said. "And now… my focus is my son. I want to give him a better future. I want him to be proud of me."

The words sounded rehearsed. Responsible. Heavy.

Dinner stretched longer than planned. They remembered more than they should have. The years between them folded inward.

When they left the restaurant, neither of them said goodbye.

The hotel was close.

Selene went with him.

Upstairs, conversation faded. The world outside narrowed. The rules that once defined them no longer applied. They were adults now. Wounded. Choosing each other without pretending there were no consequences.

In the morning, the city woke quietly.

Adan stood by the window, already distant in posture if not in body.

They didn't talk about what came next.

They didn't need to.

When they parted later that day, Selene believed something fundamental had shifted. That the waiting had finally meant something.

For the first time, she thought the bond might have found its place in the real world.

She didn't yet understand the cost of that hope.

CHAPTER NINE

The Promise

The truth came out faster than Selene expected.

Marco noticed the distance first. The way she moved through rooms without fully arriving. The way her phone stayed closer than usual. The way silence followed her like something unfinished.

He didn't ask twice.

When Selene told him, she didn't soften it. She didn't dramatize it. She spoke plainly, the way people do when they already understand the consequences.

Marco listened without interruption.

Then he told her he was leaving.

There were no accusations. No raised voices. Just a quiet recognition that something essential had shifted beyond repair.

The divorce moved quickly. There were no long arguments. No drawn-out negotiations. Just paperwork, decisions, and the quiet dismantling of a life that had once felt earned.

Selene became a single mother almost overnight.

She held herself together because she had to. For her child. For her job. For the version of herself she had fought to become. There was no room for collapse.

Adan came back to her city not long after.

This time, he was single.

The divorce he had spoken about was finalized now. There was no wife in the background. No marriage complicating the truth. For the first time, Selene allowed herself to believe the bond could exist without interference.

She felt relief. Lightness. The sudden release of something she hadn't realized she was still carrying.

They spent time together openly. No rules. No hiding. No Mrs. White watching from doorways.

Selene thought this was what freedom felt like.

It wasn't.

Adan loved her. That part was real. He didn't deny it. He showed it in moments—careful words, attentive presence, the way his focus stayed with her when they were together.

But love wasn't enough.

Fear traveled with him.

So did obligation.

His son anchored every decision. Every plan bent toward proximity, routine, and consistency. He had built his identity around staying where he was, no matter what it cost elsewhere.

He went back to his town.

This time, it wasn't his mother holding him there.

It was the same pattern, wearing a different name.

Selene understood the logic.

In practice, it broke something clean.

She saw then that Adan was not her rescue. Not her reward for surviving. Not the ending that justified the waiting.

He was her final lesson.

She stood alone again, holding a life she had built piece by piece—altered, but intact.

The moon rose that night, full and indifferent.

Selene looked up out of habit.

Hello, moon.

This time, the words didn't ache.

They settled.

Some bonds don't end because love disappears.

They end because choosing each other requires courage neither person is willing to claim.

CHAPTER TEN

Distance That Breathes

Selene tried one last time to choose courage over habit.

She didn't beg. She didn't plead. She spoke carefully, the way people do when they've already survived enough loss to recognize desperation when it shows up.

She told Adan they could do it differently.

That they didn't have to repeat the mistakes handed down to them. That their children didn't have to grow up inside the same patterns of absence and restraint. She told him she was willing to move. Willing to be there for him. For his son. For whatever this could look like if they stopped living around fear.

She offered him a future that didn't require running.

Adan listened quietly.

He always did.

He didn't interrupt. He didn't dismiss her. His face stayed calm, thoughtful, burdened in the way men look when they already know the answer but wish they didn't.

"What is stopping us?" Selene asked finally.

The question didn't come sharp. It came tired.

"All you care about is that I'm okay," she said. "When I do well in life, you're there. You're excited for me. You support me. You're proud of me."

She paused, steadying herself.

"But I don't understand this," she continued. "We're too old to keep going back and forth. Either I'm available and you're with someone, or you're available and I'm with someone. Time never aligns."

Her voice lowered.

"Why can't we make it work if we truly love each other?"

Silence followed. The kind that pressed instead of answered.

"Why keep this connection between us?" she asked. "If my mother was wrong about us being twin flames, then fine. We can break that. We can forget about each other."

The words hurt to say, but she said them anyway.

"But you don't," she added quietly. "You keep coming back. You open old wounds. You say just enough to make me believe there's still something here."

Adan looked away before he spoke.

"I have a duty now," he said. "My son. My country."

She waited.

"I signed a twenty-year commitment," he continued. "I need to serve. I need to finish what I started."

The words sounded practiced, like something he'd rehearsed alone.

"And you," he said, softer now. "You took an oath too."

Selene didn't interrupt.

"You chose to protect your community," he said. "You can't just leave the badge behind. Not after everything you went through. Look how far you've come in life."

Pride threaded through his voice. Real pride. The kind that made her chest ache.

"You matter there," he said. "You built something. You're strong."

She understood what he was saying.

Duty over desire.
Service over self.
Respect framed as restraint.

He wasn't telling her no.

He was telling her why yes would cost too much.

"So we just keep doing this?" Selene asked quietly. "Serving everyone else and calling it love?"

Adan didn't answer.

Instead, distance arrived the way it always had. Slowly. Messages grew shorter. Conversations spaced farther apart. Silence reclaimed its familiar place between them.

That night, Selene couldn't sleep.

The house was quiet. Her child breathed softly down the hall. Responsibility pressed in from all sides, but her thoughts stayed fixed on the one thing that never seemed to resolve.

She reached for her phone and reminded him of the moon.

She didn't explain. She didn't have to.

His response came quickly.

"That never changed," Adan said. "It's a promise we made to each other. Through all these years, it stayed with me. I will always carry your love with me. I'll carry you wherever I go."

The words wrapped around her like reassurance and warning all at once.

They comforted her.
They confused her.

He could leave. He could choose duty. He could build a life that did not include her in any tangible way.

But he refused to release the bond.

That contradiction kept Selene suspended between hope and acceptance. It was easier to endure absence than to accept erasure.

She told herself love didn't always need proximity. That some connections existed outside conventional rules. That restraint might still be devotion.

History supported the lie.

The moon rose full that night, steady and unmoved by human confusion.

Hello, moon.

For the first time, the ritual didn't feel like connection.

It felt like a question.

Some promises don't free you.
They keep you waiting.

CHAPTER ELEVEN

Time Served

Adan left for the military.

Years passed.

He went to Afghanistan. Duty carried him farther than promises ever had. Distance hardened into routine. Silence became normal.

Selene stayed.

She raised her child. She showed up every day. She wore the badge with intention. She chose her oath the way she chose everything else in her life—fully, without shortcuts.

She became a good cop. A steady one. The kind people trusted. The kind who didn't flinch under pressure.

Life moved forward because it had to.

Eventually, Selene met someone new. A caring man. Patient. Present. He understood her work. He respected her boundaries. He didn't compete with her past, and he didn't try to erase it.

She thought, maybe this is it.

They married.

They didn't have children together. They didn't need to. What they shared was quieter than longing—partnership, stability, mutual regard.

He loved her well.

And still, something remained.

Selene didn't speak Adan's name. She didn't invite him into conversations or arguments or quiet moments. But occasionally, he appeared anyway—a photo online, a uniform, a caption about service and sacrifice.

She never reached out.
Neither did he.

When contact was possible, timing never aligned. He was deployed. She was working. Life stayed just out of sync, as if habit itself were in charge.

Selene didn't want Adan back.

She wanted peace.

She wanted to understand why broken promises echoed louder than fulfilled ones.

At night, when the world slowed, the moon still found her.

Hello, moon.

She said it without hope now. Without expectation.
Just acknowledgment.

Some loves don't pursue you loudly.
They linger quietly.

And sometimes, surviving them takes longer than surviving everything else.

—

Adan did not talk about Afghanistan when he came home.

He answered questions efficiently. Where he went. How long he stayed. That he was fine.

People heard what they wanted to hear.

The truth was quieter.

War didn't arrive all at once. It settled in slowly long days under an unforgiving sun, nights where sleep came in fragments, the constant awareness that something could go wrong without warning.

Fear became background noise.

The first time he lost someone, he told himself it was part of the job. The second time, he stopped trying to explain it. By the third, his body learned something his mind hadn't caught up to yet.

Attachment was dangerous.
Care created hesitation.
Hesitation killed people.

So, Adan learned to wait. To observe. To delay reaction until certainty arrived.

Certainty rarely came.

That lesson followed him home.

In Afghanistan, he survived by suppressing instinct. By letting orders replace desire. By treating emotion as a liability.

Back home, there were no orders telling him how to love.

Selene wrote during those years. Letters at first. Then messages. Then silence.

He told himself the distance was necessary. That he would reach out when things settled. That there would be time later.

Time became something he stopped trusting.

He watched marriages collapse around him. Heard men speak about love like it was risk management. Like exposure.

So he waited.

Waiting felt responsible.
Waiting felt safe.

The irony never occurred to him.

PTSD didn't announce itself with explosions and breakdowns. It arrived as numbness. As avoidance. As a future that felt unreliable.

Selene represented a future.

A life that required choice instead of reaction.

That terrified him.

When his mother offered control disguised as stability, he accepted it. When someone else made decisions for him, he mistook relief for peace.

The battlefield changed.

The conditioning didn't.

Adan never learned how to come back.

He only learned how to survive.

And survival, he would understand too late, is not the same thing as living.

CHAPTER TWELVE

What Remains

Selene had built a full life.

A career shaped by discipline and choice. A child who anchored her to the present. A husband who showed up without conditions. A life that held, instead of asked.

And still, San Solano lived somewhere inside her.

Not as longing.

As history.

She no longer wondered what might have been. She no longer searched for signs or alignment. What remained was quieter than hope—an imprint left by something that had shaped her before she knew how to choose.

She understood that now.

Love had not stayed because it was unfinished.

It stayed because it was never allowed to begin.

That distinction mattered.

In San Solano, Adan finally spoke the truth he had spent a lifetime deferring.

He told his mother about Selene. About the years. About the bond that had survived silence and distance and duty.

He spoke about wanting to reach out. About wondering if naming the truth might free him.

Mrs. White listened.

Then she shook her head.

“Let her be,” she said calmly. “You’ve already taken enough from her.”

She showed him pictures.

Selene smiling. Selene settled. Selene standing inside a life that did not include him.

“She is happy,” Mrs. White said. “That is not something you get to disturb.”

For the first time, Adan did not argue.

Not because he agreed.

But because he finally understood.

Love that required silence to survive was not love he could offer without harm.

Obedience had taught him how to endure.

It had never taught him how to choose.

That night, Selene lay awake beside her husband, listening to the steady rhythm of a life she had built deliberately.

The moon rose, full and familiar.

She looked up.

And for the first time, she did not speak.

No greeting.
No ritual.
No promise.

The moon did not disappear.

It simply became what it had always been.

A witness.

Not a tether.

Distance settled—not as loss, but as space.

Space where memory could exist without instruction.
Space where love no longer asked for sacrifice.
Space that finally allowed her to breathe.

Some connections are not meant to be carried forward.

They are meant to be understood.

And understanding, Selene learned, is how love finally let's go.

CHAPTER THIRTEEN

What Took Hold

Time did not rush them toward answers.

It moved steadily, indifferent to unfinished stories, pulling days into years without asking permission from memory or regret.

Selene continued her life with precision. Her career demanded focus. Her child demanded presence. Her marriage required a kind of honesty she was still learning—not because she lacked love, but because part of her had been shaped long before vows or titles.

She was good at what she did.

At work, she led with calm authority. She trained younger officers. She carried herself with confidence earned through experience, not ego. People trusted her judgment. They felt safe around her.

At home, she showed up. She cooked. She listened. She laughed when laughter was appropriate. She loved her husband in ways that were steady and real, even when they were not uncomplicated.

There were moments when she felt divided.

Not between two men.

Between whom she had been
and who she had chosen to become.

Adan no longer occupied her thoughts the way he once had. She didn't replay conversations. She didn't imagine reunions. The urgency had thinned, replaced by something quieter.

Recognition.

Love, she understood, did not always end cleanly. Some love finished its work and stepped aside without ceremony.

She stopped checking his life. Not as a decision. As a shift. Curiosity softened into distance. Memory loosened its grip.

In San Solano, Adan experienced something similar.

Life settled into structure. Service shaped his days. Fatherhood anchored his priorities. He had learned how to live with discipline and how to contain what could not be corrected.

War had taught him how to survive silence.

Time taught him something else.

Selene was not the life he failed to choose.

She was the life that taught him how much choice mattered.

Mrs. White aged quietly.

Time softened her presence without erasing her authority. The certainty she once carried gave way to a quieter watchfulness she never named.

One evening, she found Adan sitting alone, the television on but unwatched.

She looked at him for a long moment.

Then she said nothing.

That was how Adan knew something had finally ended.

Not love.

Permission.

Selene felt the change too.

Not as grief.

As relief.

One night, after a long day, she stepped outside and stood beneath the open sky. The neighborhood was quiet. The air cool.

The moon rose full and steady.

She noticed it.

And kept breathing.

For the first time, she didn't speak.

No greeting.
No ritual.
No meaning assigned.

The moon didn't disappear.

It simply existed.

Selene understood then that the bond had never asked her to wait.

It had never required sacrifice, restraint, or loyalty at the cost of herself. It had shaped her—and then released her.

Some connections are not meant to last forever.

They are meant to teach you how to live fully afterward.

Selene went back inside and closed the door behind her.

Not in sadness. In peace.

CHAPTER FOURTEEN

Out of Alignment

Adan did not talk about the war.

He carried it instead.

The nights were the hardest. Sleep came in fragments. Sudden sounds lingered long after they passed. His body stayed alert even when there was nothing left to protect.

He told himself he could handle it alone.

That was how he had learned to survive.

The bar became a place where noise softened memory. Where dim lights blurred the edges of days, he didn't know how to enter sober. He went often enough to be noticed.

That was when Jezebel saw him.

She was older than she looked. Careful with her appearance. Botox smoothed time from her face, but not from her eyes. She watched before she spoke. Measured before she moved.

A single mother of four, she knew how to read people. She had learned survival differently.

She noticed his schedule. The nights he came alone. The way he drank slowly at first, then faster. The way he kept his back to the wall.

She waited.

When she finally spoke to him, it felt accidental.

It wasn't.

Jezebel met Adan at his most vulnerable. She listened. She flattered. She offered comfort without asking questions he didn't want to answer.

She made him feel chosen.

Slowly, carefully, she attached herself to him.

What felt like attention became control. What felt like care became monitoring. She wanted to know where he was. Who he spoke to. What he said.

She read his messages. Checked his phone. Decided who belonged in his life and who didn't.

Selene was a threat.

Not a friend.
Not a memory.

A danger.

Jezebel sensed the history immediately. The depth. The unfinished nature of it. The way Adan's body shifted when Selene's name surfaced.

So she closed the door.

Any attempt Adan made to reach Selene was met with anger, fear, or threat. Jezebel and Mrs. White—knowingly or not—reinforced the same instruction.

Leave her alone.
Let her be.
Move on.

Adan complied.

He wanted peace.

PTSD does that. It narrows the world until compliance feels like safety.

Jezebel's grip tightened.

His drinking increased. What began as escape became dependence. His discipline slipped. His work suffered. The clarity that once defined him eroded under exhaustion and alcohol.

The life he had built unraveled.

The house went first. Then the routine. Then the momentum. Then the man he had been.

He moved in with Jezebel.

Isolation followed quickly. She kept him away from family. From friends. From anyone she believed might remind him who he had once been.

Jezebel was afraid.

Afraid of being abandoned.
Afraid of aging.
Afraid that if Adan remembered himself, he would leave.

Her fear hardened into control.

Adan's disorder worsened. Anxiety deepened. Alcohol filled the spaces therapy never touched because he never sought it.

He mistook possession for loyalty.
Control for care.
Silence for peace.

He did not realize he was sealing his fate.

Some people do not fall because they are weak.

They fall because they are wounded and desperate for quiet.

And sometimes, the worst damage is done by the person who promises to make the noise stop.

CHAPTER FIFTEEN

The Mark

They never spoke about it openly.

That was the agreement.

No explanations. No witnesses. No stories passed down to anyone else. What bound them did not need language to survive.

The tattoos came years earlier, during one of the brief moments when life felt suspended instead of closing in. Nothing elaborate. Nothing obvious. A small, intentional mark placed where only they would know to look.

A symbol of permanence without possession.

They promised to keep it secret.

Not because they were ashamed. Because some bonds lose their power once they are explained.

When Selene arrived in San Solano for training, she didn't announce herself.

Officially, it was routine. Required. Temporary.

Unofficially, something in her had known she needed to be there.

When Adan found out, the coincidence felt too sharp to ignore.

They met quietly, away from familiar streets. Away from places Jezebel frequented. The moment they saw each other, something light broke through the tension that had followed them for years.

For the first time in a long while, they laughed.

Real laughter. The kind that pulls you backward before you can stop it.

At dinner, they talked like they used to. Childhood memories. Dumb jokes. Moments that only made sense to them. Time loosened its grip. The weight lifted, just enough.

Later, they ended up at the tattoo shop.

It wasn't planned.

It felt remembered.

They stood side by side, flipping through designs, pointing, debating placement like teenagers sneaking something sacred into the world. They chose together. The same mark. The same place.

When the needle started, Selene watched Adan's face instead of her own arm. When it was his turn, he did the same. They took pictures. Short videos. Proof not for the world, but for the days they might doubt this ever happened.

They smiled in those images.

Not the practiced kind.

The real kind.

The phone buzzed.

Once.

Then again.

And again.

Jezebel.

Calls stacked. Messages followed. Demands sharpened into accusations.

Adan turned the phone face down.

Fear crossed his face, and Selene understood immediately.

Not fear of being caught.

Fear of what Jezebel might do.

They finished quickly after that. The mark complete. The moment sealed.

Outside, the night closed around them.

Selene stopped him.

"There's something you need to know," she said.

He waited.

"My training here isn't random," she said. "I joined an undercover task force. This isn't just career advancement. It's dangerous."

Adan's posture changed instantly.

"If anything, ever happens to me," Selene continued, steady and deliberate, "I appointed you as guardian over my child."

The words landed harder than anything else that night.

"You trust me with that?" he asked quietly.

"I trust you more than anyone," she said.

Something broke open in him.

Not romance.

Responsibility.

Faith.

Legacy.

"I'll get help," he said without hesitation. "Sobriety. Therapy. Whatever it takes."

His voice didn't waver.

"I want to be someone your son can look up to," he said. "I want to be worthy of that trust."

Another promise formed between them.

Not about love.

About survival.

They parted carefully. No kisses. No dramatic goodbyes. Just a long look and an understanding neither needed to explain.

Later, alone, Selene touched the tattoo and felt the full weight of what it meant.

The mark did not promise happiness.

It did not promise togetherness.

It promised responsibility.

Some bonds are not about staying.

They are about standing up when it matters most.

CHAPTER SIXTEEN

The Cost of Belief

By the time Selene reached this point in her life, she was no longer guessing who she was.

The task force demanded precision. She moved through shadows now, operating in spaces where trust was currency and mistakes were unforgiving. Her days blurred into long stretches of controlled risk. Her nights were quiet, guarded, deliberate.

She was good at it.

Danger sharpened her instincts. Purpose steadied her hands. She believed in the work, even when it required parts of herself to remain unseen.

Adan was trying to rebuild at the same time.

From a distance, Selene could see the effort. Therapy appointments. Meetings he didn't always want to attend. Periods of sobriety followed by setbacks he never named publicly. Growth that wasn't linear or impressive, but real.

Some days, they spoke.

Short messages. Check-ins. Updates about exhaustion, progress, work. A quiet I'm proud of you exchanged without ceremony.

Other days, there was nothing.

Silence returned without explanation, and Selene had learned not to pursue it.

She could always tell when Jezebel was present.

Not because Adan said anything.

Because Jezebel tagged him.

Photos appeared suddenly. Carefully framed smiles. Public declarations designed to look effortless. Adan never posted on his own.

Jezebel did it for him.

Selene understood the intent immediately.

Jezebel knew Selene watched from a distance. She knew exactly who the audience was. The posts were curated. Strategic. Built to suggest happiness where stability was thin.

Look at us.
Look how settled he is.
Look how unnecessary you are.

But Selene didn't read captions.

She read eyes.

In every photo, Adan looked diminished. Not abused. Not broken.

Absent.

Loneliness sat behind his gaze. Compliance softened his posture. The man she had known was buried beneath adaptation.

Selene began asking herself questions she had avoided for years.

What kept them together?

It wasn't love.
It wasn't joy.
It wasn't growth.

And slowly, the realization settled.

Life wasn't complicated.

People made it that way.

They chose fear, familiarity, and avoidance — then blamed timing or fate when those choices hollowed them out.

For the first time, Selene questioned her mother's readings.

She had been told her entire life that she and Adan would end up together. That the bond was inevitable. That twin flames always found their way back.

But no one had ever explained how.

No one had named the cost.

No one had said in which world that ending existed.

One night after training, Selene stood alone, the city spread beneath her. The moon rose full and unchanged by human confusion.

Hello, moon.

The words no longer carried expectation.

They carried understanding.

Maybe the reading wasn't wrong.

Maybe it belonged to another lifetime.
Another set of choices.
Another version of them.

Some destinies don't fail.

They simply require courage neither person is willing to claim.

And understanding that hurt less
than believing forever.

CHAPTER SEVENTEEN

The Confession

Maribel opened her eyes and looked at her daughter.

"I need to confess something," she said.

Selene leaned closer.

"I regret ever forming the bond between you and Adan," Maribel continued. "I regret it more than anything I have ever done."

The words settled heavily in the room.

"I did it before you were born," Maribel said. "Before you had a voice. Before you had a choice. I believed I was protecting something sacred. I believed I was giving you a gift."

Her breath caught, then steadied.

"But I was wrong."

Selene did not interrupt.

"I have watched your life unfold," Maribel said. "Your marriages. Your pain. Your strength. I have watched Adan's life unravel from a distance. And through all these years, you both still cared for each other without knowing how to stop."

Her voice trembled—not with fear, but with grief.

"You have been living inside a story I started," Maribel said. "Trying to be happy. Trying to be whole. Carrying something that never belonged to you."

Tears gathered in Selene's eyes, but she stayed still.

"It has been painful to witness," Maribel continued. "To see you both endure instead of choose."

She closed her eyes for a moment.

"I can offer a way to release it," she said. "Not through magic. Not through fate. Through permission."

Selene swallowed.

"I know you don't believe in spiritual explanations," Maribel said softly. "You believe in discipline. Choice. Responsibility."

Selene nodded.

"But if you want freedom," Maribel said, "try believing in yourself once. Not in destiny."

She reached beneath the blanket and placed a folded piece of paper in Selene's hand.

"The words aren't power," Maribel said. "They are closure. A way of telling your body and your mind that the story has ended."

Her gaze drifted toward the doorway.

"I hope Mrs. White releases her son," she said quietly. "She believed control was love."

Her voice weakened.

"It caused harm," Maribel said. "He needed freedom. You both did."

Footsteps sounded behind Selene.

She turned as Adan entered the room.

He had driven through the night when he heard the news. Grief moved faster than reason.

He stopped just inside the doorway.

"I heard everything," he said softly. "I didn't mean to."

Maribel smiled faintly.

"You needed to," she said.

Adan stepped closer, emotion tightening his chest. He had always respected Maribel. She had been warmth in his life when everything else felt conditional.

"I will try," he said. "For both of us."

Maribel nodded, relief easing her expression.

"That is all I ever wanted," she said. "Peace for you both."

She reached for his hand with what strength remained. He took it carefully.

"You were a good son to me," she said. "Always."

Tears slipped down his face.

"I loved you," he said. "I always will."

Maribel's breathing slowed. Her grip loosened. Her face settled.

She rested.

The room grew still.

Selene and Adan stood side by side without touching.

For the first time, nothing stood between them.

No myth.
No secrecy.
No future demanding obedience.

Only truth.

"We should let it go," Adan said quietly.

Selene nodded.

Not with certainty.

With intention.

Later, alone, Selene unfolded the paper in her hand. She read the words without reverence and without fear.

Freedom would not come from breaking a bond.

It would come from refusing to carry a story that no longer belonged to her.

Maribel rested in peace.

And for the first time, Selene believed peace might be possible too.

CHAPTER EIGHTEEN

The Night We Tried to Let Go

Maribel's funeral was simple.

No spectacle. No mystery. No whispered interpretations of signs. Just a quiet gathering of people who had known her as a mother, a neighbor, a woman who carried too much responsibility for too long.

Selene stood near the front beside the casket, composed in the way grief sometimes demands. Her posture was straight. Her face calm. Those who approached her offered condolences and moved on, unaware of the weight settling inside her chest.

Adan stood a few rows back.

He did not approach immediately. He watched Selene instead—the strength in her stillness, the restraint in her silence. He recognized it. It was the posture of someone surviving something without falling apart.

Mrs. White sat on the opposite side of the room.

She did not look at Selene.

Not out of cruelty.

Out of avoidance—the kind that comes when truth threatens the foundation you've built your life on.

When the service ended, Selene stepped outside alone.

The sky was heavy with clouds. The air thick and unmoving. Grief pressed down without urgency, just presence.

Adan found her there.

They didn't embrace.
They didn't speak at first.

"She wanted us to try," Selene said finally.

Adan nodded. "I know."

That night, they drove separately to the place Maribel had written down.

The instructions were simple. Clear. Stripped of mysticism. Intention without performance.

The moon rose full and indifferent, as it always did.

They stood facing each other beneath it, the distance between them deliberate.

Selene took the red ribbon from her pocket. She wrapped it once around her wrist, then handed the other end to Adan. He mirrored her movements—steady hands, quiet focus.

The ribbon connected them loosely.

Not tight.
Not binding.

Symbolic.

They stood like that for a long moment, listening to the night. No cars. No witnesses. Just breath and memory.

"This isn't about punishment," Selene said. "It's about release."

"I want peace," Adan said. "For both of us."

They spoke the words Maribel had written.

Not a prayer.
Not a request.

A statement.

They acknowledged the bond. Named what it had given. Named what it had taken. Thanked it without honoring it.

Then Selene lifted the small blade.

For a moment, she hesitated.

Not because she believed something terrible would happen.

But because she wasn't sure who she would be without the bond.

"It's okay," Adan said quietly.

She cut the ribbon.

It fell between them, landing softly on the ground.

They waited.

Nothing changed.

No rush of relief.
No sudden emptiness.
No sense of freedom washing over them.

The awareness remained.
The familiarity.
The quiet recognition that had followed them across decades.

Selene exhaled slowly. "So much for rituals."

"I don't think it works like that," Adan said.

They stayed longer than planned, the moon watching without judgment.

"This doesn't mean we failed," Selene said at last. "It means this isn't something you cut away."

Adan nodded. "It's something you stop feeding."

They didn't touch.

They didn't promise.

They left the ribbon on the ground.

On the drive home, Selene felt the grief fully for the first time—not just for her mother, but for the years spent believing something else would decide for her.

Adan felt it too.

The ritual didn't break the bond.

It broke the illusion that something external would.

Maribel was gone.

What remained was choice.

And choice, Selene knew, was heavier than fate.

CHAPTER NINETEEN

After The Cut

The ritual did not follow them home.

That was the first thing Selene noticed.

There was no heaviness. No backlash. No sense that something had been awakened or disturbed. Life continued as it always had—traffic, notifications, responsibilities waiting without patience.

That unsettled her more than anything else.

If nothing changed, then nothing external had ever been holding them together.

The days after Maribel's funeral passed slowly. Selene returned to routine because routine required obedience. Work. Training. Meetings that demanded attention even when her thoughts lagged behind.

She did not reach for Adan.

Neither did he.

The silence between them was new.

Not painful.

Intentional.

For the first time, neither of them tried to soften distance with words. The failed ritual had stripped away the excuse to pretend they were waiting for something to happen.

Nothing was coming.

In San Solano, Mrs. White felt the shift immediately.

She didn't know about the ribbon or the words spoken beneath the moon. She knew absence. She knew when control loosened.

Adan stopped responding as quickly.

Not defiantly.

Quietly.

He still came home. Still fulfilled expectations. Still complied with routine. But something in him had withdrawn. The edge of obedience dulled.

Mrs. White noticed the way he stared through conversations. The way his answers shortened, less rehearsed. The way he no longer offered explanations.

It unsettled her.

She had built her life on certainty—on knowing what was best, on believing restraint equaled protection.

Adan had always accepted that.

Until now.

One evening, she confronted him in the kitchen.

"You've been distant," she said. "Is something wrong?"

Adan rinsed his cup, set it in the sink, then turned to face her.

"Maribel died," he said. "I'm processing."

Mrs. White nodded stiffly. "I know. It's sad."

It wasn't what he needed.

"She was more than sad to me," Adan said.

Mrs. White's posture tightened. "I did what I thought was right," she said. "I protected you."

Adan exhaled slowly.

"You controlled me," he said.

Not angrily.

Factually.

Mrs. White bristled. "I saved you from a mistake."

"You saved yourself from discomfort," Adan said.

Silence settled between them.

Mrs. White had no response prepared for that.

She had spent years believing interference was love. That closeness justified authority. That sacrifice on someone else's behalf required no consent.

Now, faced with the cost, she resisted the truth the way people do when identity is threatened.

"You're not thinking clearly," she said. "You've been through too much."

Adan met her gaze.

"I'm thinking clearly for the first time."

That frightened her.

Control rarely loosens gracefully. It tightens before it breaks.

After that, Mrs. White withdrew. Polite. Distant. Cold. She spoke less and watched more. She told herself she had done nothing wrong. That time would prove her right.

But doubt had entered.

And doubt does not leave quietly.

Selene experienced the shift differently.

Without ritual to blame, responsibility landed squarely on her. The bond no longer felt mystical or sacred. It felt familiar. Conditioned. Sustained by memory and avoidance.

She saw it clearly.

Love had not trapped them.

Fear had.

The moon rose full again a week later. Selene noticed it without ceremony. Without greeting. Without meaning attached.

That felt like progress.

She thought of Maribel then. Not with anger. With compassion. Her mother had meant well.

That did not erase the harm.

Good intentions were not protection.

They were choices.

In San Solano, Adan sat alone one night after another argument he didn't start and didn't finish. He felt the familiar urge to reach out, to explain himself to Selene, to soothe discomfort.

He didn't.

For the first time, he let the feeling pass without action.

The bond didn't disappear.

But it weakened.

Not because of scissors or words or moonlight.

Because neither of them fed it.

Mrs. White sensed the change but could not stop it.

Some control lasts only as long as compliance does.

And something in Adan had finally stepped out of reach.

CHAPTER TWENTY

Almost

There was a year when Selene and Adan existed in each other's lives again without truly being in them.

Not through grand gestures.
Not through confessions.

Through drafts that were never sent. Calls that rang too long. Messages typed late at night and deleted before morning.

Selene noticed it first.

She would wake in the dark with her phone in her hand, the screen glowing softly. His name sat there, untouched, like a question she no longer trusted herself to ask.

Sometimes she typed.

I was thinking about you.
I hope you're okay.
Do you ever wonder—

She erased every version.

She had learned where wondering led.

Adan felt it too, though he never named it. He scrolled through old photos he pretended not to remember saving. He lingered on her social media longer than he admitted to himself. He read articles about police work and thought of her without letting the thought finish.

They orbited each other from a distance, pulled by gravity neither of them fully believed in anymore.

Once, Adan did call.

It rang until voicemail.

Selene heard the missed call hours later, standing in her kitchen with the radio low and her uniform half undone after a long shift.

She didn't call back.

Not because she didn't want to.

Because she knew how easily one conversation could reopen something she had fought hard to contain.

That night, she dreamed of the field where they used to sit as teenagers. The truck was there. The moon was full.

Adan never arrived.

She woke with her chest tight and an unfamiliar clarity settling in.

She could survive without answers.

That realization frightened her more than longing ever had.

Months later, Selene ran into someone who knew Adan casually. A shared connection from long ago. His name surfaced without warning.

"He's been through a lot," the person said. "Seems tired."

Selene nodded politely, as if the information were neutral.

Later, alone in her car, she rested her forehead against the steering wheel and closed her eyes.

She wondered how two people could feel so close and remain so separate.

How many lives were lived in the space between almost and never.

Adan sat on the edge of his bed one night with a bottle in his hand and Selene's contact open on his phone.

He didn't drink.

He didn't call.

He watched the screen dim and go dark.

"I don't know how to do this," he whispered.

That was the truth he never said aloud.

He didn't know how to move toward something without destroying it.
He didn't know how to choose without losing someone else.

So he did what he had always done.

Nothing.

Selene eventually stopped checking her phone.

Not dramatically. Gradually.

Life required her attention elsewhere. Work intensified. Training expanded. Responsibility grew heavier. The part of her that used to wait learned how to stay occupied.

She told herself that was growth.

And maybe it was.

But some nights, when exhaustion stripped away discipline, she admitted something quietly.

Almost hurt more than never.

Because almost left the door unlocked.

And doors left open too long become dangerous.

The year passed without resolution.

No reunion.
No closure.
No final argument.

Just silence shaped by hesitation on both sides.

Selene didn't know it then, but that silence would become permanent.

And Adan would spend the rest of his life understanding exactly what he lost by waiting for certainty in a world that never offered it.

CHAPTER TWENTY-ONE

What She Never Said Out Loud

Selene had learned how to function while unraveling.

That skill came from years of practice. Years of showing up when she wanted to disappear. Years of smiling through exhaustion because vulnerability invited questions she didn't have the energy to answer.

Her colleagues admired her composure. They called her steady. Reliable. Unshakeable.

They didn't see the nights when she sat alone in her kitchen long after midnight, uniform folded neatly on the chair, staring at nothing with a drink untouched in her hand—not because she wanted it, but because she was afraid of what it would mean if she did.

They didn't know how close she had come to not stopping.

Alcohol had crept into her life quietly. A way to soften the edges after long shifts. A way to sleep without replaying scenes that refused to stay in the past.

At first, it felt manageable.

Then it wasn't.

The pills came later. Prescribed. Justified. Meant to help. Taken together, they blurred the line between coping and escaping.

Selene noticed before anyone else did.

She always did.

That was the hardest part—knowing, watching herself slip, and still needing to function.

She stopped drinking alone one night without telling anyone. Poured everything down the sink. Sat on the floor afterward, shaking, furious with herself for needing something so badly.

Marco had been the first person to see through her armor years earlier. He helped her believe survival didn't require silence. Therapy followed. Meetings she rarely spoke in. Accountability without spectacle.

She stayed sober not because it was easy.

Because she had a child watching her.
Because she wore a badge that demanded clarity.
Because she refused to let pain be the thing that defined her.

And still, in the quiet moments, her thoughts drifted where she told herself they wouldn't.

Adan.

Not as he was.

As what he represented.

The unfinished sentence of her life.

She hated herself for that sometimes. Hated that after marriages, abuse, healing, and success, her mind still returned to the boy who never chose her.

She wondered if something was wrong with her.

She wondered if love was supposed to hurt this long.

On nights when the moon was full, she stepped outside and said hello without expectation.

No response.
No fantasy.

Just acknowledgment.

She didn't believe in twin flames the way her mother had taught her.

But she believed in patterns.

And some patterns, she had learned, took a lifetime to unlearn.

Selene chose duty because it was solid. Predictable. Honest.

Love had never been any of those things.

Her shift began the way most of them did.

Quiet.

The city looked calmer under artificial light, but she knew better. Darkness didn't create chaos.

It hid it.

She parked her unit and stepped out before logging in. The air was cool. Still. The moon hung full and unapologetic above the rooftops, bright enough to cast shadows.

She tilted her head back and smiled faintly.

"Hello, moon," she said.

It wasn't a ritual anymore.

Just habit.

She thought about her son earlier that evening—the way he laughed when she teased him about his schedule. How independent he had become.

He didn't need her the way he once had.

Instead of pain, the thought brought pride.

That was how it was supposed to be.

She logged in and began her patrol.

Routine calls. A noise complaint. A traffic stop that ended with a warning. A check on a closed business.

Selene liked nights like this.

They gave her space to think.

She thought about the woman she used to be—afraid, compliant, quiet in ways that had nothing to do with peace.

She remembered the first time she put on a uniform and felt taller inside it. Defined. Present in her own body instead of waiting for permission.

She had loved fiercely.
Had failed.
Had survived things she once believed would end her.

And still, here she was.

Whole.

Her radio crackled. She answered calmly. Logged the call. Drove on.

She didn't think about Adan actively anymore.

He lived in her the way old music lived—familiar, emotional, not disruptive unless invited.

When the moon was full, memories surfaced gently.

Not longing.

Recognition.

She remembered sitting in a field years ago, dust on her jeans, Adan beside her, both of them young and unaware of how heavy life would become.

She remembered talking about the moon and love and distance and connection.

She smiled.

"You were wrong," she whispered. "But it's okay."

She wasn't angry at that girl anymore.

She was grateful.

Selene parked again near a quiet street and shut off the engine. She leaned her head back against the seat and closed her eyes for a moment.

Her body felt tired.

Not exhausted.

Just present.

She breathed slowly.

This life had not given her everything she wanted.

But it had given her enough.

Enough strength.
Enough purpose.
Enough clarity to know she had lived honestly—even when the truth hurt.

Her radio interrupted her thoughts.

A warrant service. Routine. Address confirmed. Backup en route.

"Copy," she replied.

She started the engine and pulled away from the curb.

As she drove, she glanced once more at the moon through the windshield.

"Looks like the crazies will be out tonight," she said softly.

There was no fear in her voice.

Only awareness.

She parked, stepped out, adjusted her vest. Her movements were practiced, calm, exact. She checked her surroundings, listening to the distant hum of the city breathing.

This was her world.

She walked toward the door with steady steps.

Selene did not know this was the last night of her life.

But she felt no unfinished business pressing against her chest.

No panic.

No regret.

Only the quiet certainty of a woman who had finally stopped waiting.

CHAPTER TWENTY-TWO

Under a Full Moon

Selene had always preferred the night shift.

The city told the truth after dark. People stopped pretending. Fear surfaced. Anger sharpened. Desperation moved closer to the skin. At night, motives were louder and lies were thinner.

She liked that.

She adjusted her vest as she stepped out of the car, the air cool against her face. The neighborhood was quiet in the way that never meant safe. Porch lights flickered. A dog barked once, then went silent.

She looked up.

The moon was full.

Bright. Unapologetic.

Selene smiled faintly and shook her head. "Hello, moon," she said under her breath. "Looks like the crazies will be out tonight."

Her partner glanced at her and smiled. "You always say that."

"And I'm always right," Selene replied.

The warrant was routine.

On paper.

Mid-level offender. Prior violence. Known to flee. Known to carry. The task force had cleared it carefully. Entry planned. Backup staged. Every box checked.

Selene had served hundreds of warrants.

This one felt no different.

Until it did.

They approached quietly. Radios low. Breathing steady. Selene's body shifted into the familiar state where fear receded, and training took over. Her movements were precise. Her mind clear.

She knocked.

"Police," she called. "Search warrant."

Silence.

She knocked again. Louder.

Movement inside.

"Police," she repeated.

The door burst open.

Everything happened at once and not at all.

A body surged forward. A flash of metal. A sound so sharp it fractured the night.

The impact hit her before thought could catch up.

Her chest seized. Air vanished. The ground rushed up and met her hard, the pavement cold against her cheek.

Pain followed.

Immediate. Consuming.

Her partner shouted. Weapons raised. Chaos erupted. Footsteps scattered as the shooter ran.

Selene tried to move.

Her body didn't respond.

She lay still, stunned by how quiet everything suddenly felt, as if sound itself had pulled away.

"Selene," someone shouted. "Stay with me."

She wanted to answer.

She couldn't.

Her vision blurred, then cleared just enough for her to see the sky.

The moon was still there.

Full. Bright. Unchanged.

A calm settled over her—not peace, not comfort, but focus. Breathing became deliberate. Each inhale counted.

She fixed her gaze upward.

Hello, moon.

The words stayed inside her.

Images surfaced—not panic, not regret. Just memory arranging itself gently.

A life she never lived.

A kitchen filled with morning light. A version of Adan older, quieter, unburdened. Laughter without tension. Evenings that ended without exhaustion.

No secrecy.
No interference.
No waiting.

It didn't hurt.

It didn't tempt.

It simply existed.

Then faded.

She understood it for what it was.

Possibility.

Not loss.

This was the life she hadn't chosen.

And she did not resent the one she had.

Hands pressed against her. Voices layered. Sirens approached, growing louder.

She was lifted onto a stretcher. Pain flared, sharp and insistent. Her eyes fluttered open, then closed again.

The moon disappeared as they loaded her into the ambulance.

For a brief moment, she wondered if Adan would look up tonight.

The hospital arrived in fragments.

Light. Motion. Commands. Pressure.

She drifted.

Her son's face surfaced—older now, steadier. The thought that he would be okay brought relief.

She wasn't afraid.

Somewhere, far away, her phone rang.

Her son's hands shook as he held it.

He called Adan.

Once.

Twice.

Jezebel answered.

"There's been a shooting," he said, breathless. "My mom. Selene. She's been shot. She's at—"

Jezebel didn't respond.

She ended the call.

Then she blocked the number.

Adan slept on.

Back in the trauma bay, Selene's body fought quietly. Treatment helped. Then didn't. Numbers dipped. Stabilized. Dropped again.

A nurse leaned close and spoke softly, though she didn't know why. "You're not alone."

Selene didn't hear her.

But she wasn't alone.

In her fading awareness, a memory surfaced—not a bond, not a pull.

A voice.

Adan's. Years earlier.

I will always carry you with me.

She smiled faintly.

Maybe he did.

If he had been told, he might have come.

He might have held her hand.

He might have spoken her name.

Or it might have made leaving harder.

She would never know.

The doctor called the time.

The room went still.

Selene died as she had lived.

On duty.

Clear-eyed.

Faithful to her oath.

The news broke before sunrise.

A decorated officer. A respected task force member. A woman known for composure and integrity under pressure.

Her name filled screens.

Her face followed.

The nation watched.

Tributes came quickly. Vigils. Folded flags. Officers standing in silence.

For days, her story led every broadcast.

Adan woke to her face on the television.

The world tilted.

He stood motionless as the anchor spoke words that refused to settle.

Officer Selene was killed in the line of duty last night…

His chest tightened painfully.

He reached for his phone.

No missed calls.

No messages.

Only silence.

The moon had already set.

CHAPTER TWENTY-THREE

The Funeral

The city shut down for her.

Adan understood that the moment he stepped out of his car and saw the sea of uniforms stretching farther than his eyes could follow. Officers from across the country stood in formation—state troopers, county sheriffs, federal agents, local departments. Patches he didn't recognize stitched onto dark blue sleeves worn with absolute reverence.

Thousands of them.

They lined the avenue in two perfect parallel rows, forming a corridor of bodies and badges.

An avenue of honor.

No one spoke.

The hearse approached slowly, escorted by motorcycles moving in tight precision. As it passed, every officer snapped to attention.

Present arms.

The sound was sharp. Unified. Final.

Adan felt it land in his chest.

The casket was draped in the American flag. Thirteen folds pressed flat and exact. Selene's cap rested on top, her badge placed beside it, as if she might return to claim them.

She would not.

Bagpipes began to play as the casket was lifted. The sound carried long and low, grief given form. Not comforting. Just honest.

Adan stood near the back among civilians dressed in black. He did not belong among the uniforms. Not here. Not after everything.

Helicopters passed overhead.

Three.

One broke formation and veered upward.

Missing man.

Adan closed his eyes.

Inside the church, the honor guard moved with practiced precision. Every step measured. Every turn deliberate. This was ritual, but not hollow. It was discipline shaped by respect.

Selene's life reduced to ceremony.

But honored.

The service unfolded without dramatics. Speakers talked about her composure under pressure. Her leadership. Her integrity. Words like duty and service were spoken carefully, as if volume might cheapen them.

Adan listened, but his thoughts drifted.

He remembered her laugh. Her stubbornness. The way she held herself when she was exhausted but refused to show it.

He remembered the moon.

Outside, the rifle squad took position.

Three volleys.

The cracks split the air, sharp and echoing. Each shot landed like punctuation at the end of a sentence no one wanted to finish.

Then the bugle.

Taps.

The notes rose and fell, fragile and final. The sound carried across the crowd, across the ranks of officers standing motionless, across a city that would continue without her.

Something inside Adan broke completely.

The final radio call followed.

A dispatcher's voice, steady and reverent.

"Officer Selene Rivas, badge number 1814."

The number echoed.

Silence.

No response.

The dispatcher spoke again, softer.

"Officer Selene Rivas… last call."

The radio clicked.

Nothing answered.

That silence was louder than the rifles. Louder than the bagpipes. Louder than grief.

The flag was folded next.

Slowly. Precisely. Thirteen movements into a perfect triangle. Each fold carried weight.

The honor guard turned and approached Mathew.

He stood straight. His face set. Older than he should have been.

They knelt and presented the flag.

Mathew accepted it with both hands.

Then he turned.

And walked directly toward Adan.

He stopped in front of him.

"You're Adan," Mathew said.

Adan nodded. "I'm sorry—"

"What did you get out of it?" Mathew asked.

Adan froze.

"All those years," Mathew continued. "What did you get out of being my mother's shadow?"

People nearby pretended not to hear. Some did hear and stayed still.

"She spent her life trying to be enough," Mathew said. "Smart enough. Strong enough. Worthy enough."

Adan swallowed.

"She loved you," Mathew said. "Quietly. Patiently. Without demanding anything."

His jaw tightened.

"And you let her," Mathew said. "You let her live like that while you chose someone else."

Adan opened his mouth.

Mathew didn't stop.

"You chose Jezebel," he said. "Someone who controlled you because she was afraid you'd leave. Someone so insecure she erased anyone who mattered before her."

The words landed cleanly. Without heat.

"My mother spent her life believing in something better than what she was given," Mathew said. "And you let her."

Adan's eyes filled. He did not wipe them.

"I was there," Mathew said. "When she was tired. When she doubted herself. When she broke quietly. You were just an idea she kept alive."

He extended the folded flag.

"You need this more than I do."

Adan stared at it, unable to move.

"I knew her," Mathew said. "You lived in her hope."

Silence stretched.

"I hope you carry it," Mathew said quietly. "For the rest of your life."

He turned and walked away.

Adan remained standing, the folded flag heavy in his hands.

Unbearable.

Selene was buried with honors.

Adan left alone.

That night, the moon rose full again.

For the first time, Adan could not look at it.

CHAPTER TWENTY-FOUR

What Was Left Behind

Adan didn't leave the cemetery right away.

The crowd thinned slowly. Officers peeled away in quiet groups. Engines started. Radios crackled back to life. The world resumed movement as if nothing permanent had happened.

Selene stayed buried.

He stood near the edge of the grass, the folded flag heavy beneath his arm. He hadn't planned to keep it. He hadn't planned anything beyond the moment Mathew pressed it into his hands.

The words replayed without mercy.

Shadow.
False hope.
Illusion.

They followed him like a sentence without punctuation.

When he finally drove home, the house felt wrong. Too loud in its silence.

Jezebel was waiting.

She sat upright on the couch, hands folded, eyes sharp with expectation.

"You disappeared," she said.

He didn't answer.

"You embarrassed me," she continued. "People were asking where you were."

Adan stopped in the middle of the room.

"She died," he said.

Jezebel waved a hand dismissively. "People die every day."

Something detached inside him then.

Not anger.

Clarity.

"You answered the phone," he said quietly.

She stiffened. "What phone?"

"My phone," Adan said. "When her son called."

Silence stretched.

"You blocked the number," he said.

Jezebel stood. "I protected you."

Adan let out a short laugh. Empty.

"You protected yourself," he said.

Her voice rose. Excuses poured out — fear disguised as devotion, control framed as care. She spoke quickly, desperately, as if volume could reverse what had already ended.

Adan didn't argue.

He sat down instead.

That frightened her.

"She died alone," he said. "And you decided I didn't deserve to know."

"She chose that life," Jezebel snapped. "She chose danger over you."

Adan looked up.

"No," he said. "I chose you."

The words settled between them.

"And this is the result."

Jezebel froze.

Adan stood and walked past her into the bedroom. He packed slowly. Methodically. Like a man dismantling something already dead.

She followed — pleading, then threatening, then crying. Bargaining with a future that no longer existed.

He didn't stop.

By the time he left, the sun was rising.

Adan drove until the city blurred. He pulled over at a quiet overlook and turned off the engine.

For the first time in his life, there was no one telling him what to do.

No mother.
No Jezebel.
No Selene.

Just silence.

He pressed the folded flag to his chest and felt the full weight of what he had lost.

Not Selene.

The chance to choose her when it mattered.

Some losses don't come from death.

They come from delay.

CHAPTER TWENTY-FIVE

No One Left to Carry It

Adan did not sleep.

Not the first night.
Not the second.

When exhaustion finally forced his eyes closed, his body startled awake minutes later—heart racing, breath shallow, the room unfamiliar despite the cracks in the ceiling he had already memorized.

He had left Jezebel's house with nothing but a duffel bag and the folded flag.

That was all he owned now that mattered.

He rented a small room on the edge of town. Bare walls. A thin mattress. One chair by the window. The kind of place meant for people passing through.

Adan stayed.

Days lost their shape. Without Jezebel's surveillance, without his mother's expectations, without Selene's quiet presence anchoring him somewhere in the world, time stretched in uncomfortable ways.

He tried sobriety again.

Meetings. Paper cups. Folding chairs. Stories that sounded too familiar to be coincidence.

He spoke once.

"I waited too long," he said.

No one asked what he meant.

They didn't need to.

PTSD did not leave when the people around it disappeared. It settled deeper. Sounds sharpened into threats. Silence pressed harder than noise.

At night, Adan sat on the floor with his back against the bed, the folded flag beside him. He did not unfold it.

He was afraid of what it would mean if he did.

He thought about Selene constantly now.

Not how she died.

How she lived.

Her discipline. Her resolve. The way she chose service even when it cost her rest, comfort, and connection. The way she loved without asking to be chosen in return.

He understood too late that her love had never been a request.

It had been an offering.

The moon rose full again one night.

Adan sat by the window and stared at it until his eyes burned.

"I'm sorry," he said aloud.

The words went nowhere.

Mrs. White called eventually.

Her voice sounded smaller now. Less certain.

"You shouldn't be alone," she said.

Adan didn't answer.

"I did what I thought was right," she added.

"So did she," Adan said quietly.

Silence followed.

His health began to slip without ceremony. Missed meals. Too much alcohol on nights when sleep refused to come. Medication forgotten. Appointments skipped because explaining himself felt unbearable.

No one intervened.

No one rescued him.

That was the truth he had spent his life avoiding.

Selene had lived knowing no one was coming to save her.

She had shown up anyway.

Adan had waited his entire life for permission.

Now there was no one left to give it.

One night, he folded the flag tighter, pressing the creases flat with shaking hands.

"This is what's left," he whispered.

Not love.

Responsibility.

Some people survive loss.

Others are finally forced to face it without distraction.

Adan sat alone in the dark, understanding for the first time that grief does not end when you accept it.

It begins when you have nowhere else to place it.

CHAPTER TWENTY-SIX

What He Numbed

Adan started drinking again without ceremony.

There was no declaration. No moment of decision. It returned quietly, the way habits do when resistance wears thin.

One drink became two. Two became something he stopped counting. Painkillers filled the gaps alcohol couldn't reach — leftovers from old prescriptions, refills he never questioned. Pills swallowed without water, without pause.

Sleep came easier that way.

So did forgetting.

By then, his mother was gone.

Mrs. White passed not long after Selene. The timing felt cruel, almost intentional, as if the world were closing doors in sequence. Adan attended the service alone. No speeches lingered. No conflicts revisited. Whatever authority she once held dissolved with her.

He felt relief.

He felt guilt for feeling it.

His son had moved away years earlier. Grown into a man Adan admired from a distance — an architect now, stable, grounded, designing structures meant to last. They spoke occasionally. Carefully. Polite updates exchanged without depth.

Adan did not ask him to come back.

He would not ask anyone to anchor him again.

Jezebel left without spectacle.

He discovered the affair accidentally — a message left open, a name he didn't recognize, conversations that made no effort to hide what they were. The realization didn't hurt.

It clarified.

She had never loved him.

She had possessed him.

And even that had limits.

When he confronted her, she didn't deny it.

"You were never really here," she said.

She was right.

She packed and left the same day.

Adan watched her drive away without regret.

He felt something close to gratitude.

They had never married. Never signed anything binding. Only promises spoken in moments of fear and loneliness.

Promises made to avoid being alone.

He was alone now.

And there was an honesty in that.

The nights stretched long and heavy. Adan sat at the small kitchen table in his rented apartment, bottles lining the counter like markers of time passing. He stared at nothing, his thoughts drifting backward without resistance.

What could have been.

He imagined Selene at this age. Smile lines. A tired laugh. The way she would have criticized his drinking without cruelty.

He imagined mornings that never happened. Arguments that would have mattered. Growing old without constantly negotiating silence.

The visions didn't torment him.

They exhausted him.

Because now he knew exactly where everything had gone wrong.

Not at the beginning.

At every moment he chose safety over courage.

He poured another drink. Took another pill.

The flag remained folded on the shelf above the sink.

He never moved it.

Some nights, he spoke to Selene aloud.

Not prayers.

Not apologies.

Observations.

"I finally understand," he said once. "Too late."

The moon rose full outside the window.

He didn't greet it.

The ritual was over.

Memory stayed.

Adan drank until the edges softened. Until thought slowed. Until regret became manageable.

He was not trying to die.

He was trying to survive without feeling.

That distinction mattered less as time passed.

The world continued without him.

And Adan remained — suspended between what was and what never would be, numbing himself against a future that no longer asked anything of him.

CHAPTER TWENTY-SEVEN

The Envelope

Mathew didn't go through his mother's things right away.

He handled the obvious first—paperwork, benefits, the badge retirement, the meetings where people kept using the word closure like it meant something.

Grief didn't respect schedules.

When he finally returned to her apartment, the silence felt wrong. The air still carried her shampoo, coffee, fabric softener. Her boots waited by the door as if she might step back into them.

Mathew moved slowly, not because he feared what he'd find, but because everything he touched felt final.

In her closet, behind a row of uniforms pressed too neatly, he found a small lockbox.

Not hidden.

Placed.

Inside were a few carefully wrapped items—a spare badge clip, a small notebook with dates and case numbers, photographs of Mathew as a child. And a folded piece of paper in Maribel's handwriting.

Beneath it lay an envelope.

Thick. Cream-colored. Sealed.

On the front, in Selene's clean, familiar script:

Adan.
If I don't make it home.

Mathew stared at the name until his throat tightened.

He didn't open it.

He knew immediately it wasn't meant for him. But the fact that it existed felt like a betrayal.

Even in death, she had left room for Adan.

Mathew sat on the edge of her bed, the envelope heavy in his hand. Anger came fast—hot, protective.

He thought of the flag. Of Adan standing there holding it like something he hadn't earned.

He thought of the unanswered call. The hospital. The time that could have been.

He thought of the years his mother had carried Adan quietly, like a private ache she refused to name.

Mathew stood and paced the room.

He wanted to tear the envelope open. To destroy it. To protect his mother from loving someone who never chose her.

But Selene had been many things.

Careful. Disciplined. Loyal.

And stubborn.

If she wrote this, she meant it.

Mathew carried the envelope to the kitchen table and stared at it for a long time. He imagined her writing it late at night after a shift. Tired. Steady. Practical.

The same woman who trained for danger.

The same woman who still looked up at the moon.

He remembered a night from childhood when he caught her outside, eyes on the sky.

"Who are you talking to?" he'd asked.

She smiled like she didn't want to answer.
"No one," she said. "Just a habit."

Mathew understood now.

It hadn't been a habit.

It had been hope.

He hated that.

He hated that she died carrying a love she never got to live. Hated that Adan still occupied space in her story.

Mathew lifted the envelope again.

Adan. If I don't make it home.

He laughed once. Sharp.

Even in death, she made room for him.

Mathew decided then.

He would give it to Adan.

Not as kindness.

As consequence.

It took one phone call to get the address. People still treated Selene's son gently. Still felt responsible.

Mathew drove to San Solano with the envelope on the passenger seat.

No music.
No stops.

He drove like he was delivering evidence.

When he knocked, it took a long time for the door to open.

Adan looked thinner. Older. His eyes dulled, like a man who had been underwater too long.

Mathew didn't greet him.

He held out the envelope.

"She wrote this," he said. "Before she died."

Adan stared at it like it might burn him.

Mathew leaned closer.

"If you open it," he said quietly, "you open it alone. You don't get to turn her into a story."

Adan's hands trembled as he took it.

Mathew turned and walked away.

He didn't look back.

The Letter

Adan,

If you're reading this, I didn't make it home.

I'm not writing to haunt you. I know you'll try to carry guilt like it's a job. You'll let it destroy you because you think you deserve it.

You don't get to destroy yourself in my name.

You don't get to make my death your excuse.

You were not the reason I lived.
You were not the reason I served.
You were not the reason I became who I became.

I chose my life.

Yes, I loved you. That's true. It didn't fit cleanly into the life I was living. I'm not proud of it. I'm not ashamed of it. It just was.

But love is not the same as choice.

And you did not choose me.

That sentence used to hurt. Now it feels like honesty.

I made peace with it—not because it was fair, but because I couldn't keep carrying a story that never moved forward.

The moon ritual was mine. It helped me survive years that demanded more than I had. It was never your responsibility.

If you stayed away because you thought it was right, I understand.
If you stayed away because you were afraid, I understand that too.

Fear is powerful.

It kept you in places you didn't belong.
It kept me waiting longer than I should have.

But I stopped waiting.

If I died on duty, I died doing what I believed in. There is nothing romantic about that. Do not turn my death into a love story.

This was a life.

My son is grown. He is good. He does not need saving. Do not try to become his father out of guilt.

If you want to honor me, do this:

Get help.
Stop drinking.
Stop mixing pills with pain you refuse to name.
Stop letting fear make your decisions.

Choose something once in your life and stand in it.

Not for me.

For you.

I am at peace.

I hope you find yours before it takes you.

— Selene

Adan couldn't breathe.

He lowered the letter to the table, hands shaking. He leaned forward, palms flat against the wood, holding himself in place.

He read it again.

Slower.

When he reached This is not a love story, he flinched.

Because he had tried to make it one.

The bottle sat within reach.

He stared at it.

Then he stood and poured it out.

The smell rose sharp as the liquid vanished down the drain. His body protested. His hands clenched.

He poured out the rest.

He dumped the pills into the toilet and watched them dissolve.

This wasn't courage.

It was desperation.

He didn't want to die like this.

He called his son.

"I need help," he said.

"I'm coming," his son replied. "You're going to rehab."

"Okay," Adan whispered.

He sat on the bed with the letter in his hands.

Outside, the moon rose.

"Hello, moon," he said, breaking.

Pain seized his chest without warning.

Sharp. Crushing.

He tried to stand.

His knees failed.

He hit the floor hard, the letter slipping from his fingers. He dragged it back to his chest like a folded flag.

His last breath left him in a sound that almost formed her name.

Then the room went still.

CHAPTER TWENTY-EIGHT

What Remains

The news did not travel far.

Adan's death made a brief mention in the local paper. A few lines buried between community notices and weather updates. A man found alone in his apartment. Natural causes complicated by years of damage no one noticed soon enough.

There was no honor guard.
No bagpipes.
No final call.

His son arrived two days later.

He stood in the doorway of the small apartment and took it in quietly—the emptiness, the stale air, the sense that the space had been waiting to be cleared rather than lived in.

On the table lay a letter.

Selene's handwriting was unmistakable.

Adan's son did not open it.

He folded it carefully and placed it back where it had been, understanding instinctively that some words were not meant to be inherited.

He packed what mattered.

Very little did.

The folded flag rested on the shelf above the sink. He hesitated before lifting it, then held it carefully, feeling its weight.

Not pride.

Responsibility.

In another city, Mathew stood at his kitchen counter holding a cup of coffee gone cold.

He had already buried his mother.
He had already said everything he needed to say.

When he heard about Adan, he felt nothing at first.

Then something loosened.

Not forgiveness.

Release.

Two sons.
Two different losses.
Neither of them asked for what they inherited.

Mathew stepped outside and looked up.

The moon was thin that night. Not full. Not commanding.

Just there.

He thought of his mother standing under it years ago, speaking to it like it could hold what she never said aloud.

For the first time, Mathew understood her.

Not the ritual.

The need.

Across the state, Adan's son stood by a hotel window, the folded flag resting on the bed.

He had come too late to save his father, just as Adan had come too late for Selene.

Patterns were cruel like that.

He did not blame Selene.

He did not blame his father.

He blamed the space between choices—the years where fear spoke louder than truth.

Time passed.

The world moved forward the way it always does.

Selene's name lived on in plaques and training rooms and quiet stories told to new recruits. Officers spoke of her with respect, with admiration, with a sense of loss that never fully faded.

Adan's name faded faster.

That was not unfair.

He had lived his life in waiting.

The moon continued its cycle—full, thin, hidden, revealed.

No rituals followed it now.

No promises tied to its light.

Only memory.

And memory, unlike fate, eventually loosens its grip.

This was never a love story.

It was a lesson.

Love without choice becomes longing.
Duty without balance becomes isolation.
Waiting too long becomes a life.

Some bonds are not meant to be kept.

They are meant to teach.

And when the lesson is finally learned, peace does not arrive with noise.

It arrives quietly.

Like the moon.

Always there.

Never waiting.

CHAPTER TWENTY-NINE

What People Call a Bond

People called it many things.

Twin flames.
Soul ties.
Destined connections.

Language meant to explain why certain people lingered in the mind long after logic said they shouldn't.

Selene had never liked the words.

They made suffering sound romantic.

After her death, stories about her circulated quietly. Officers spoke of her strength. Her discipline. Her steadiness under pressure. A few—those who had known her longer—mentioned the man she never fully released.

Adan's name surfaced in whispers.

Not accusations.
Not praise.

Curiosity.

Mathew heard it once at a gathering he hadn't wanted to attend.

"She and that man had a bond," someone said. "You could feel it."

Mathew didn't respond.

He had watched his mother live inside that bond. Had seen what it cost her. Had seen how belief turned patience into obligation and absence into virtue.

If that was a bond, he wanted nothing to do with it.

Months later, Adan's son thought about it too, standing alone in his father's apartment before it was cleared out.

He found no letters between them.
No photographs framed on shelves.
No evidence of a connection people insisted had defined his father's life.

Only absence.

If bonds were real, he thought, they left strange proof.

Maribel had believed fiercely. She spoke about connections as if they were contracts written before birth. She had wanted meaning in a world that rarely offered it.

She had meant well.

But meaning, Selene learned, did not require destiny.

It required choice.

People confused intensity with inevitability.
Confused familiarity with permanence.
Confused longing with love.

Selene and Adan had felt deeply.

That much was true.

But feeling was not the same as building.

What they shared was not a flame meant to burn forever.

It was a mirror.

They saw in each other the lives they were afraid to claim. The courage they admired but postponed. The versions of themselves they believed existed only in another timeline.

The bond did not trap them.

Belief did.

Belief said waiting was noble.
That patience proved love.
That timing mattered more than action.

Years disappeared inside that story.

Whole lives.

Selene eventually stepped out of it.

Adan did not.

That was the difference.

After their deaths, no signs appeared. No dreams delivered answers. No moon glowed brighter than usual.

The world remained indifferent.

And somehow, that was comforting.

Because it meant there was no cosmic cruelty at play. No universe conspiring to keep them apart.

Only two people shaped by fear, duty, love, and hesitation.

Only choices.

People like stories where suffering has purpose.

But sometimes suffering is simply what happens when people do not choose each other in time.

That truth is harder than fate.

Because it offers no one to blame.

CHAPTER THIRTY

What Love Is Not

People talk about love as if it is rare.

As if finding it is the hardest part.

Selene learned the opposite.

Love was everywhere.

It arrived early. It lingered. It returned in different forms wearing familiar faces. Love showed up in friendships, in motherhood, in purpose, in service, in moments so ordinary they were easy to miss.

What was rare was courage.

Courage to choose love when it asked for action instead of patience. Courage to speak when silence felt safer. Courage to disrupt comfort in favor of truth.

Selene had loved deeply.

She had also learned how easily love became an excuse.

An excuse to wait.
An excuse to forgive absence.
An excuse to endure uncertainty longer than was healthy.

Adan loved her too.

But love, Selene understood too late, was not the problem.

Indecision was.

People confuse intensity with depth. They confuse longing with connection. They confuse familiarity with destiny.

And then they stay.

They stay in half-relationships. In emotional holding patterns. In lives that feel unfinished because finishing them would require risk.

Selene had lived long enough to see the cost of that.

Love that is not chosen becomes weight.

Love that is not acted on becomes memory.

Love that is delayed becomes regret.

She wished she had learned sooner that clarity is kinder than hope without follow-through. That being almost chosen is more damaging than being rejected outright.

Adan never meant to hurt her.

That was the tragedy.

Harm does not require intention.

It requires avoidance.

Selene had eventually chosen herself. Chosen duty. Chosen integrity. Chosen a life that was solid, even if it was not complete in the way she once imagined.

Adan never made that shift.

He kept believing that love alone would carry him forward. That circumstances would align. That time would soften what fear hardened.

Time does not soften anything.

It only reveals.

The lesson Selene left behind was not about twin flames or fate or cosmic bonds.

It was simpler.

If someone loves you but will not choose you, that is information.

If someone keeps you waiting, they are already making a choice.

If love feels like suspension instead of movement, something is wrong.

You do not need permission to walk away from what hurts you.

You do not need destiny to justify choosing yourself.

And you do not need to stay loyal to a story that keeps you small.

Selene learned that.

Adan did not.

That difference shaped everything that followed.

CHAPTER THIRTY-ONE

The Lives That Continued

Life did not pause for their absence.

It rarely does.

Selene's son returned to his routine slowly. Back to work. Back to mornings that no longer included a text reminding him to eat or drive carefully. He learned how to carry grief the way adults do when no one is watching.

He kept her picture on his desk.

Not the one in uniform.

The one where she was laughing, hair loose, eyes soft.

That was how he chose to remember her.

Over time, he spoke her name less—not because she mattered less, but because saying it no longer felt like survival. It felt like continuity.

He built a life she would have been proud of.

And that mattered.

Adan's son did the same.

He returned to his city. To blueprints and deadlines and meetings where no one knew his father's story. He kept the flag folded and stored away, not out of shame, but out of respect.

He understood something his father never fully had.

You could love someone and still choose to live differently.

He did not inherit the weight.

He inherited the lesson.

The two sons never met again.

They did not need to.

Their connection existed only because of two people who could not figure out how to choose each other in time. That was not a bond meant to be carried forward.

It ended with them.

Selene and Adan became stories told quietly.

Her name lived on in honor rolls, training rooms, and memory walls. His name faded into private remembrance, held by fewer people as years passed.

That was not injustice.

That was consequence.

The moon continued to rise.

Some nights full.
Some nights hidden.
Some nights barely there at all.

No one spoke to it anymore.

No promises were tied to its light.

No meaning was demanded from it.

It simply existed.

Just like the truth.

Selene and Adan were not punished by fate.

They were shaped by choices.

They loved.
They hesitated.
They waited.

And life continued without them.

This was not a story about destiny denied.

It was a story about time misunderstood.

And the quiet truth that sometimes the greatest tragedy is not losing someone—

It is never fully choosing them while you still can.

Afterword

Good Night, Moon

This book exists because Selene trusted me with her story.

I am grateful I was allowed to witness her strength, her contradictions, and the quiet ways she carried love and loss. Watching her move through duty, heartbreak, healing, and resolve shaped how this story was told.

This was never meant to be a romance.

It was meant to be honest.

I wrote this book in the hope that someone reading it might pause. Might recognize themselves. Might see where waiting has disguised itself as loyalty, or where longing has been mistaken for love.

Time moves quickly.

And for Selene and Adan, it moved without mercy.

It's natural to wonder what might have happened if Adan had chosen her sooner. Maybe the ending would have been joyful. Maybe ordinary. Maybe difficult in ways that had nothing to do with destiny.

But that question misses the truth of their story.

This is not about what could have been.
It's about what was delayed too long.

Sometimes what feels like love is not love at all.

Sometimes it is fear.
Sometimes it is habit.
Sometimes it is a bond that keeps you suspended instead of alive.

Real love does not require disappearance.
It does not demand endurance as proof.
It does not ask you to shrink.

Real love chooses.
It shows up.
It moves forward with you.

If you see yourself in these pages, I hope you look at your life with kindness and clarity. There may already be people who are choosing you without hesitation. There may be a life waiting that does not require you to disappear to earn it.

Time is not infinite.

Choose courage over waiting.
Choose clarity over confusion.
Choose yourself when love asks you to vanish.

Selene's story was lived.
Adan's story was lived.

Yours is still unfolding.

Until our next book.

Good night, moon.

Reader Resources

This story explores themes that may resonate deeply with some readers, including trauma, abuse, addiction, grief, and mental health struggles. If you or someone you know is affected by similar experiences, support is available.

Immediate Help

If you are in danger or experiencing a mental health crisis, please contact your local emergency services.

Mental Health & Crisis Support (U.S.)

- 988 Suicide & Crisis Lifeline
  Call or text 988 | www.988lifeline.org
  Free, confidential support 24/7

Domestic Violence Support (U.S.)

- National Domestic Violence Hotline
  Call 1-800-799-SAFE (7233) | Text START to 88788
  www.thehotline.org

Substance Use & Addiction Support (U.S.)

- SAMHSA National Helpline
  Call 1-800-662-HELP (4357)
  www.samhsa.gov/find-help
  Free, confidential treatment referral and information service

PTSD & Trauma Support

- National Center for PTSD (U.S. Department of Veterans Affairs)
  www.ptsd.va.gov

If you are outside the United States, local health services, crisis lines, or international organizations can help connect you with appropriate resources in your area. Seeking support is a sign of strength. You do not have to navigate difficult experiences alone.

Acknowledgments

This book exists because of the courage it takes to tell the truth quietly.

I am grateful to those who trusted me with pieces of their lives, their memories, and their experiences, even when those stories were difficult to revisit. Your honesty mattered.

Thank you to the readers willing to sit with discomfort, to question familiar narratives, and to consider the cost of waiting. Stories like this only have meaning when they are met with openness.

And to those who choose courage over silence, clarity over fear, and action over delay—this book is for you.

About the Author

Jennifer Montiel is a police officer and writer whose work explores themes of duty, trauma, love, and the consequences of delayed choice. She has served in law enforcement since 2011 and brings firsthand insight into the emotional weight of service, resilience, and responsibility.

Her writing is grounded, reflective, and shaped by lived experience rather than idealized outcomes. This novel examines how fear, belief, and silence can shape lives just as powerfully as action.

Jennifer lives with her family and continues to serve her community while writing stories that center honesty, accountability, and human complexity.

Made in the USA
Coppell, TX
21 January 2026

68942685R00075